Fairies Welcome

A SURPRISE FOR WILLOW

By Bea Jackson

Simon Spotlight

New York   Amsterdam/Antwerp   London
Toronto   Sydney/Melbourne   New Delhi

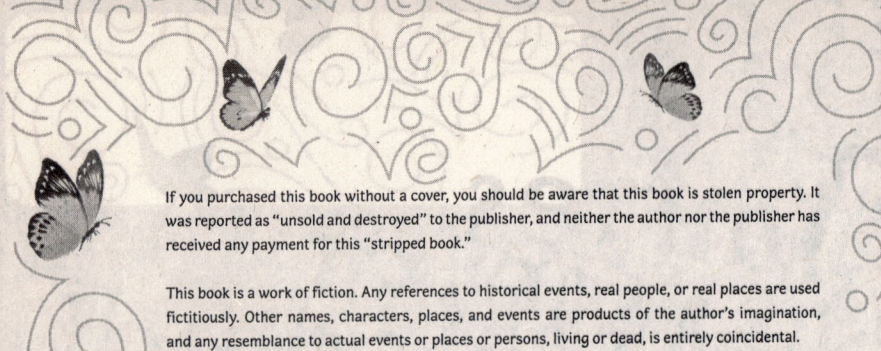

If you purchased this book without a cover, you should be aware that this book is stolen property. It was reported as "unsold and destroyed" to the publisher, and neither the author nor the publisher has received any payment for this "stripped book."

This book is a work of fiction. Any references to historical events, real people, or real places are used fictitiously. Other names, characters, places, and events are products of the author's imagination, and any resemblance to actual events or places or persons, living or dead, is entirely coincidental.

SIMON SPOTLIGHT
An imprint of Simon & Schuster Children's Publishing Division
1230 Avenue of the Americas, New York, New York 10020
For more than 100 years, Simon & Schuster has championed authors and the stories they create. By respecting the copyright of an author's intellectual property, you enable Simon & Schuster and the author to continue publishing exceptional books for years to come. We thank you for supporting the author's copyright by purchasing an authorized edition of this book.
No amount of this book may be reproduced or stored in any format, nor may it be uploaded to any website, database, language-learning model, or other repository, retrieval, or artificial intelligence system without express permission. All rights reserved. Inquiries may be directed to Simon & Schuster, 1230 Avenue of the Americas, New York, NY 10020 or permissions@simonandschuster.com.
This Simon Spotlight paperback edition January 2026
© 2026 by Brittany Jackson
Also available in a Simon Spotlight hardcover edition.
All rights reserved, including the right of reproduction in whole or in part in any form.
SIMON SPOTLIGHT and colophon are registered trademarks of Simon & Schuster, LLC.
For information about special discounts for bulk purchases, please contact Simon & Schuster Special Sales at 1-866-506-1949 or business@simonandschuster.com.
Simon & Schuster strongly believes in freedom of expression and stands against censorship in all its forms. For more information, visit BooksBelong.com.
The Simon & Schuster Speakers Bureau can bring authors to your live event. For more information or to book an event, contact the Simon & Schuster Speakers Bureau at 1-866-248-3049 or visit our website at www.simonspeakers.com.
Book design by Chrisila Maida
The text of this book was set in Capucine.
Manufactured in the United States of America 1125 LAK
10 9 8 7 6 5 4 3 2 1
CIP data for this book is available from the Library of Congress.
ISBN 9781665941099 (hc)
ISBN 9781665941082 (pbk)
ISBN 9781665941105 (ebook)

CONTENTS

Chapter One:

1

Chapter Two:

11

Chapter Three:

21

Chapter Four:

33

Chapter Five:

45

CHAPTER 1

"Race you to the big oak tree!" Lily called to her friends, flapping her shiny wings and soaring into the air.

"No fair! I wasn't ready!" protested Sky.

"Oh, Sky, you always say that," giggled Jasmine.

It was a beautiful spring day in Fairy Forest. The perfect spring day for Lily and her fairy friends to practice flying. First, they did wing spins, then they did rocket twirls, and now they were zipping as fast as they could toward the gnarled old oak tree at the edge of the clearing.

Lily loved the old oak tree. When she stood on certain branches, she could see the whole forest and beyond. She could see the pond with the croaking frogs. She could see the bluebirds in their nests. And she could even see her human friend Willow's house with its cheery red chimney.

"I won!' shrieked Sky when she reached the tree, grabbing onto a branch where Lily was already perched.

"How do you figure that?" Lily asked. "I'm already here."

"Well, then it's a tie because you had a head start," Sky insisted.

Lily was about to protest when she spotted something strange off in the distance. It looked like a supersized butterfly with arms and legs. And it was coming their way!

The three fairies huddled together to watch the odd creature move closer and closer until it stopped directly under the oak tree.

In a soft voice the creature began to sing.

> "We are butterflies,
> we bloom in spring,
> we flap, we flutter
> our colored wings!"

Then it began to run in circles around the base of the tree.

Suddenly Lily began to laugh. She knew that voice. It wasn't a creature after all. It was her good friend Willow! Lily floated down to the ground, followed closely by the other two fairies.

"Willow!" she called. "What are you doing? And why are you dressed up in that outfit?"

Startled, Willow came to an abrupt stop. "I didn't know anyone was watching me! I'm so embarrassed. I'm practicing for Spring Day at our school," she told the fairies. "Tomorrow we're putting on a show in the courtyard. I'm one of the butterflies. I'll be singing a song while I pretend to fly."

"That sounds like fun," said Sky.

Willow bit her lip. "But what if I forget the words? And what if I don't look like I'm swooping or soaring?" she said, worried.

Lily landed on Willow's shoulder and gave her a comforting pat with her wing. "It's okay," she said. "We can help!"

For the rest of the afternoon the fairies helped Willow memorize her song. Lily even called one of her butterfly friends to show Willow how to flutter and flap her wings gracefully.

Finally, it was time for Willow to go home. "I wish I could bring you all with me tomorrow," she said. "You are my lucky charms!"

That night Lily remembered the golden anklet her mother had given her for luck. That gave her an idea. What if the fairies went to school with Willow the next day?

"She did say we are her lucky charms," Jasmine agreed.

"And I'm a super fast flyer, remember," Sky told her friends.

"We can call it Operation Surprise Willow!" Lily shouted.

The plan was set.

CHAPTER 2

Early the next morning, the fairies reviewed the plan.

"Number one: Sneak into Willow's bag," said Jasmine.

"Number two: Surprise her when she gets to school," Sky added.

"And number three: Watch her smile when she sees her lucky charms," Lily concluded.

At Willow's house, the fairies peered through the kitchen window.

Willow was eating breakfast.

"Yummy, pancakes." Sky drooled.

Lily and Jasmine giggled. Sky loved food almost as much as she loved flying.

"Forget the pancakes, Sky," Lily said. "It's go time. Follow me!"

The fairies slipped unnoticed through the open kitchen window.

Sky sniffed the air, smelling the sweet scent of the syrupy pancakes, and looked at the breakfast table. "I wonder what Willow is having for lunch," she said, licking her lips.

Then she spotted Willow's purple backpack lying on the floor near the girl's feet. "That's it!" she buzzed. "I think I found our ride."

While Willow hugged her grandmother goodbye, the fairies darted inside the open lunch bag, using the napkin for cover. Lily held her breath as the bag was snapped shut and attached by a clip to the purple backpack.

And then they were outside, bouncing along in the lunch bag as Willow headed for school on her bike.

"Hang on!" Lily called, grabbing onto a container of carrots.

Jasmine clutched a bag of chips.

"I think she's hitting every bump in the road!" Sky complained. Her arms were wrapped tightly around an apple.

At that moment Sky noticed a flap at the top of the lunch bag. "Woohoo!" she yelled into the wind, sticking her head outside.

Cautiously, Lily and Jasmine joined their friend. A blur of houses and leafy green trees zipped by as Willow pedaled down the hill.

Before long they arrived at Woodside Elementary School. Willow parked her bike, and once inside, she skipped down the hall to her classroom. She hung up her jacket and placed her lunch bag in her cubby.

The fairies watched as Willow sat down with two other girls at a small table.

"Hey, Willow," the girls greeted her, smiling. "Ready for Spring Day?"

Willow nodded. But she looked nervous.

"Wait till she sees her lucky charms are here to cheer her on," Lily whispered.

The fairies grinned, imagining their friend opening her lunch bag.

In class Willow's teacher, Ms. Grace, took attendance. After that the students took turns reading a story out loud. The story was about a mouse and a motorcycle. It was so funny that Lily had to cover Sky's mouth when she accidentally let out a snort of laughter.

Suddenly, a loud *clang! clang! clang!* rang out. In a flash the fairies dove back into the bag.

"What's happening?" Jasmine said, eyes wide.

They heard kids laughing and talking, and one person say, "Finally, it's lunch. I'm starving!"

The fairies felt themselves being lifted into the air.

"Get ready, fairies. Looks like it's time for lunch!" Lily said.

CHAPTER 3

Lunchtime at Woodside Elementary was super noisy. Kids who were buying lunch stood in lines, banging their trays. Beeping erupted from the kitchen. A large fan whirred overhead. And everyone seemed to be shouting.

"Wow, these humans are so loud," said Sky.

"And I thought fairy festivals were wild," Jasmine agreed.

Lily, Sky, and Jasmine were so busy listening to the sounds in the lunchroom that they didn't realize Willow had unsnapped her lunch bag. She pulled out a juice box and took a sip. Then she looked down and . . .

"Aaah!" Willow shrieked, spying the fairies.

"What's the matter, Willow?" a girl at the table asked.

Startled, Willow stood up and grabbed her lunch bag. "N-n-nothing," she stammered. "I just have to go to the bathroom. Now."

The fairies hung on tightly as their friend raced down the hall and into the girls' room. Luckily, it was empty.

"Surprise!" Sky exclaimed as the three tiny pals popped out of the lunch bag and began doing wing spins around Willow.

Lily perched on the edge of the sink. Operation Surprise Willow wasn't exactly going the way she planned. Willow looked more worried than ever. And maybe even a little angry.

"What are you all doing here?" Willow demanded.

Slowly, Lily explained their plan. "We just wanted to root for you at the show," she said, hanging her head. "I'm sorry we made you mad."

"We thought we might bring you good luck," Jasmine added quietly.

Willow's face softened. "It's okay. I'm not mad," she said. "I just wasn't expecting to find you in my lunch bag . . . at school!"

"That was my idea!" Sky said proudly. "By the way, I may have taken a few tiny bites out of your apple by accident."

"By accident?" Lily teased her.

A smile spread across Willow's face. She began to giggle. The fairies joined in.

Sky was laughing so hard her wings activated the soap dispenser. Pink soap squirted everywhere. Willow grabbed some paper towels to clean up the mess. Then Lily tried to help. But when she flew under a strange metal machine, it roared to life. A strong gust of wind sent the little fairies and the paper towels flying.

"I got one!" yelled Jasmine, snatching one of the towels as it flew by.

"I got two!" shouted Sky, not to be outdone.

At that moment the door to the bathroom creaked opened. Faster than hummingbirds, all three fairies hid under the nearest sink.

A girl stood in the doorway. "Are you okay, Willow?" she asked gently, surveying the scene. "Chloe and I were worried. You missed lunch."

"Oh, uh, uh, I'm fine, Roni," Willow said, barely hiding her panic. "I'm just washing up. I'll meet you at the playground."

When the door closed, the fairies reemerged.

"I'm not sure what a playground is, exactly," said Sky. "But if it has to do with play, it must be fun!" She smiled. "Can we go?"

"We'll stay out of sight," Jasmine promised.

Lily patted Willow's shoulder. She could tell her friend was concerned someone might see them. "It's okay. We don't have to go," she said.

Willow thought for a moment. "You have to pinky promise that you won't make a sound or show yourselves. No one even knows you're real. It's just too dangerous if you are discovered."

Jasmine looked confused. "What's a pinky promise?" she asked.

Willow gathered the fairies in her palm, and wiggled her smallest finger. "Take your little fingers and tap mine, and promise you'll be careful."

The friends did as they were asked. Then Willow closed her lunch bag, scooped them up, and placed them in the pocket of her oversized sweatshirt.

"Come on," she said with a grin. "Time to show you what a merry-go-round is."

"Yay!" cheered Sky. "This fairy is ready to play!"

CHAPTER 4

With three twisty slides, twelve swings, a giant rock-climbing wall, monkey bars, a merry-go-round, catwalks, tunnels, and flying saucers, the kids at Woodside couldn't wait for recess to rush to the playground.

"Whoa!" exclaimed Sky, taking a quick peek outside Willow's pocket. "This place is amazing!"

"Just remember what Willow said," Lily whispered. "We have to stay hidden or else."

Sky nodded, but Lily could tell her fairy friend was having trouble controlling her excitement. Her wings were flapping up a storm, when they heard Mia call out to Willow.

"Willow! Over here!" Mia said. She was on a swing, going back and forth. Her shiny black hair flew out behind her as she rose higher and higher into the air. Willow raced over to her friend. She plopped down on a swing and began to pump her legs. Soon the two girls were talking and laughing as they swung together at a slow, rhythmic pace.

"This is so nice," said Jasmine.

"And relaxing," agreed Lily. "It reminds me of the leaf hammock by Fairy Lake. And it doesn't seem like Willow is that nervous, which is good."

Sky yawned. "It's okay," she said. "But I wish Willow would do something more fun. I'm falling asleep here."

But when Willow and Mia leaped off the swings, flew through the air, and landed on their feet, Sky perked up.

After the swings Willow climbed up the rock wall, dangled from the monkey bars, and whooshed down the twisty big slide again and again. Lily thought hurtling down the big slide felt like doing rocket twirls, only ten times faster.

"Come on, Mia," Willow said after the slides, and they ran over to the merry-go-round to join their class.

They started spinning slowly.

"I sure hope this ride isn't a snoozer," Sky complained.

But then the merry-go-round quickly picked up speed.

Faster and faster and faster.

The fairies clung to Willow's pocket as the world whizzed by at a dizzying speed. Even Sky was terrified!

"Help!" shrieked Jasmine as a gust of wind threatened to send her flying across the playground. Willow—along with the rest of the kids—was having so much fun, hollering with every turn, that she didn't notice her teeny friends were in trouble.

Luckily, at the last possible second, Lily and Sky each grabbed a leg, pulling Jasmine to safety.

When the ride finally stopped, the fairies each breathed a sigh of relief.

"Was that exciting enough for you?" Lily asked Sky with a grin.

Well, Lily thought, if Willow is brave enough to ride the merry-go-round at dragonfly speed, hopefully, she'll be brave enough for the show.

Back in the classroom, Mrs. Grace announced, "Okay, everyone, let's get ready. It's time for Spring Day."

Willow got her costume from her cubby. On the way back to her desk, she quietly and quickly hid the fairies behind the row of books on the windowsill.

The window looked out into the school courtyard. When the time was right, the fairies could fly out the window to the tall fir tree.

They'd have the best seat in the house to watch Willow's performance. Now they just had to stay out of sight.

CHAPTER 5

From bees to blue jays, red foxes to hedgehogs, kites to soccer balls, the class was dressed up like springtime.

Willow put on her purple and blue costume, complete with golden sparkly butterfly wings. Then she took a deep breath. "You can do this," the fairies heard her whisper to herself.

"I wish we could give her a pep talk." Lily sighed.

"Or remind her how well she did when we practiced," Sky added.

"Well, at least she'll know we're watching," Jasmine offered. "Now come on you two. The class is already headed to the courtyard. Let's go!"

Quick as larks, the fairies slipped out from behind the books and flew outside. They flitted to the top of the fir tree, settling down among the soft pine needles.

"This is perfect. No one will see us way up here," Sky said.

That's the problem, Lily thought. The fairies were so well-hidden, Willow wouldn't be able to see their smiling faces or turn to them for encouragement. And cheering was out of the question—not that anyone would actually hear their voices.

If only there was a way to send their friend a sign to let her know they cared.

The fairies watched as each class arrived. It really did look like spring was blooming all at once.

"Look, over by that rose bush, there's Willow." Jasmine pointed her out.

Lily waved, but it was no use. Willow hardly blinked.

"Welcome, students, to our Spring Day celebration," Principal Munoz announced.

And with that the performances began. One class put on a skit about Earth Day. Another danced around the courtyard, buzzing like bees.

Jasmine couldn't stop oohing and aahing at how beautiful everything was. "Which do you like better, Sky, the buttercups or the irises? I can't decide," she said.

"It doesn't really matter, because here comes Ms. Grace's class," Sky answered. "And Willow isn't looking happy at all."

"Uh-oh, her butterfly wings are sagging like she's just been in a rainstorm," said Jasmine. "She sure doesn't look like she's ready to perform—or even wants to."

Jasmine is right, Lily thought. They had to do something to help. But what?

Suddenly, she had an idea. "I know how we can send Willow a sign," she said, and let out a long, low whistle.

Within minutes a swarm of colorful butterflies filled the sky. Lily directed them down to the courtyard, where they circled Willow and then the rest of Ms. Grace's class.

It was just what Willow needed to inspire her to flutter her wings and sing her song.

"That was awesome!" Chloe said afterward. "I felt like we were in the middle of a rainbow. I wonder where those butterflies came from."

Willow glanced up at the tree and grinned. She knew exactly where those butterflies came from. She couldn't wait to thank her friends for knowing just what to do to help make her shine.

"Were you surprised?" Lily asked Willow the next day.

The friends had gathered for a picnic at Fairy Lake. They had spread out a blanket filled with mini berry tarts and almond slivers for the fairies and a cupcake and a large, shiny red apple for Willow.

"Surprised? My whole class was surprised! That was amazing!" Willow gushed. "Thanks all so much for making me feel extra-special."

The fairies beamed.

"We would do anything for you, Willow," Lily said. "You are our extra-special friend."

"And you are my extra-special lucky charms," Willow said.

"You know what else is extra-special?" Sky said after a bit. "This apple."

Lily groaned. "Oh, Sky," she said. "That apple was for Willow."

And with that, the four extra-special friends couldn't stop laughing for the rest of the afternoon.

HERE'S A SNEAK PEEK OF THE NEXT
Fairies Welcome STORY.

A Wish for Lily

One bright sunny afternoon Lily, Jasmine, and Sky soared over the treetops of Fairy Forest. They were on their way to meet their friend Willow in the lush flower garden planted by Willow's grandmother.

"There she is!" Lily called, spotting Willow sitting on a knotty pine bench next to a row of yellow honeysuckles.

excerpt from *A Wish for Lily*

Cautiously, the fairies fluttered over and hid behind a bush.

"Psst, Willow! Is the coast clear?" Sky whispered, poking her head out between the leaves.

"Oh!" Willow cried, jumping at the sight of the tiny fairy and nearly falling off the bench.

She had been so busy watching two bees buzzing around a purple crocus that she hadn't noticed the fairies' arrival.

"You surprised me again." Willow giggled.

The last time the fairies had surprised Willow, they had snuck into her lunch bag at school. It was a bit of a challenge to hide from the other students. After all, only Willow knew the fairies even existed. Still, the friends

excerpt from *A Wish for Lily*

ended up having the most exciting adventure.

Willow beamed at the fairies. "Don't worry. No one's around," she assured the group. "Grandma's in the kitchen baking plum tarts and talking to her best friend, Lila, on the phone."

At the mention of tarts, Sky licked her lips. "Yum! Plum tarts." She drooled. "Do you think she might have extras?"

Everyone laughed. Sky loved anything sweet... or salty... and everything in between.

"I'll see what I can do," Willow promised, grinning.

Just then, Lily, who had been flitting around a sweet-smelling rosebush, noticed a strange object on the ground. It had a glossy surface

excerpt from *A Wish for Lily*

with delicate coral, pink, and white swirls all over it.

"Oooh! What is that?" the fairy asked Willow. "It's beautiful!"

"That's a seashell," the girl explained to the fairies. "I found it at the beach. The ocean polished it, so it's extra shiny."

"What's a beach?" Lily asked.

"What's an ocean?" Jasmine added.

It made sense that the fairies had no idea what an ocean or a beach was. They spent almost all their lives in Fairy Forest. Plus, the nearest ocean was miles and miles away. It would take forever to fly that far with only little fairy wings for transportation.

"The beach is amazing," Willow said

excerpt from *A Wish for Lily*

excitedly. She told them about the soft, sandy dunes, the multicolored seashells, the white sand dollars, and the tiny crabs. She told them about the vast blue ocean with its frothy waves and about the dolphins and whales and other incredible creatures that lived under the sea.

When Willow was finished, Lily's eyes were huge. "It sounds like the most magical place ever," she said dreamily.

excerpt from *A Wish for Lily*